ANGRY BIRDS™ TRANSFORMERS

ROBOT BIRDS IN DISGUISE

DK

DK

LONDON, NEW YORK, MUNICH,
MELBOURNE and DELHI

Senior Editor Helen Murray
Editorial Assistant Ruth Amos
Senior Designer Guy Harvey
Design Assistant Elena Jarmoskaite
Pre-production Producer Siu Yin Chan
Producer David Appleyard
Managing Editor Elizabeth Dowsett
Design Manager Ron Stobbart
Art Director Lisa Lanzarini
Publishing Manager Julie Ferris
Publishing Director Simon Beecroft

Reading Consultant Maureen Fernandes

Rovio
Approvals Editor Rollo de Walden
Senior Graphic Designer Jan Schulte-Tigges
Publishing Director Laura Nevanlinna

Hasbro
Director of Global Publishing Michael Kelly
Senior Designer Steven Lathrop
Product Development Specialist Heather
Hopkins

First published in Great Britain in 2014 by
Dorling Kindersley Limited
80 Strand, London WC2R 0RL

10 9 8 7 6 5 4 3 2 1
001–275291–Nov/14

Page design copyright © 2014 Dorling Kindersley Limited,
A Penguin Random House Company

A CIP catalogue record for this book
is available from the British Library.

ISBN: 978-0-24118-474-5

Colour reproduction by Alta Image, UK
Printed and bound in China by South China

Discover more at
www.dk.com

Contents

ANGRY BIRDS™
TRANSFORMERS

ROBOT BIRDS IN DISGUISE

Written by Helen Murray

Welcome to Piggy Island

Piggy Island may look like
a beautiful paradise, but strange
things have happened here lately...

A mysterious power source
called the EggSpark came
crashing through the sky.
It turned the island's
birds and pigs into robots!
Even the birds' eggs grew mini
legs and became Egg-bots.

The EggSpark
This is the source
of all power
on Piggy Island.
It glows with sparks
of blue energy.

Now, the Egg-bots are
changing all the plants and
rocks into robotic objects.
Piggy Island will be destroyed!

Meet the Autobirds

Squawk hello to this heroic band of robot birds!
They are called the Autobirds.
 The Autobirds just want to nest in peace, but they have a very important mission.

Grey Slam
Grimlock Bird

Optimus Prime Bird

They must catch the Egg-bots
to stop them from destroying
the island.

They need to work with a team
of pig robots – the Deceptihogs.

Can the Autobirds trust the
greedy hogs and save their home?

Bumblebee Bird

**Heatwave the
Fire-Bot Bird**

Amazing disguises

First of all, the Autobirds must
get used to their powerful
new robot bodies.
They have arms and
legs for the first time!

Bird form

That's not all....
These robots can
switch form, too!
They can disguise
themselves as
cars, trucks and
other vehicles
whenever they want.

Robot form

The birds' vehicle modes are called their cyberforms.

The robot pigs can change into all kinds of awesome vehicle cyberforms, too.

Cyberform

Energon
Starscream Pig

Dark
Megatron Pig

The Deceptihogs

Attention! These pesky porkers
are the Deceptihogs.

They say they have united with
the Autobirds, but really they
will do anything they can to
ruffle their feathers.

The sly robot hogs are secretly trying to poach all the Egg-bots, before the Autobirds find them. The pigs plan to take them to the leader, Dark Megatron Pig, who dreams of gobbling eggs for breakfast, lunch and dinner!

Soundwave Pig

Galvatron Pig

Lockdown Pig

Optimus Prime Bird

This is Optimus Prime Bird – brave leader of the Autobirds and protector of the Egg-bots!

Fist of steel

Tough faceplate
Optimus's faceplate
is made of metal.
His pointed
audioreceptors
can hear even the
smallest piggy snort!

It is clear why Optimus is
top of the robot pecking order.
He is a skilled warrior and a
caring leader, too.

The Autobirds all look
up to wise Optimus.
It is not unusual for an excited
Autobird to short-circuit
when their hero is nearby!

Serious Optimus could never
be called the joker of the flock.
He only thinks about one thing:
catching runaway Egg-bots.
The Autobirds keep the Egg-bots
safe so they don't destroy the island.

Large exhaust pipe

Fiery
paintwork

Mean machine
Optimus changes into a powerful truck cyberform. It is perfect for hunting down Deceptihogs.

Optimus thought the robot pigs were helping the Autobirds, but he discovers the naughty porkers are kidnapping Egg-bots!

He will stop the Deceptihogs. Fire up your engines: Autobirds, roll out!

Bumblebee Bird

Who can help Optimus Prime
Bird track down the Deceptihogs?
Bumblebee Bird, that's who!
    Bumblebee is Optimus's
eager second-in-command.
He was very competitive as a
normal bird, but the EggSpark
has scrambled his brain!
Now, he just wants to be liked.
    Bumblebee is always
ready for action,
but he often drives
headfirst into danger
without thinking.

Robotic rock

Piercing
blue optics

Afterburners

No bird knows why Bumblebee
only communicates with his
radio, rather than squawking.

Speedy Bumblebee can
make quick getaways with his
lightning-fast afterburners.

Unused vocal
processor
in beak

Hidden strength
Bumblebee's chassis may not be heavy but it is incredibly strong.

Or, he can simply turn into his cyberform: a flashy sports car.

The Deceptihogs need to keep their optics peeled to spot Bumblebee Bird.

He is a blur as he zooms around the whole island in astroseconds.

Striped chassis

Grey Slam Grimlock Bird

Stomp, stomp, stomp.... Grey Slam Grimlock Bird is close by! He is a large and powerful robotic dinosaur.

Huge foot

Grimlock Bird may be strong, but he is very, very clumsy.
He often trips over his own feet.

This dinosaur is a mysterious robot and does not squawk much, but he does moan about being henpecked by Optimus.

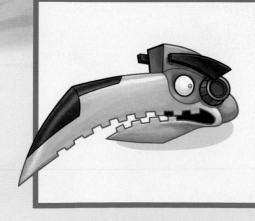

Sharp weapon
Watch out! Grimlock Bird's jagged beak can crunch straight through the toughest metal.

Wide central tyre

Grimlock Bird will always
follow Optimus, though.
In fact, this loyal fighter
follows his leader so closely,
he pokes him with his long
beak! Oops!

There is more to Grimlock
Bird than meets the beak.
He is a strong and cunning
fighter, especially when
he converts into a
motorised trike.

He whizzes past the Deceptihogs
and uses his beak to knock them off
their robotic hooves!

Heatwave the Fire-Bot Bird

Huge Heatwave the Fire-Bot Bird
is not a dainty chick – in fact,
he is a hulking lump of metal!

He is a rescue worker
known as a fire-bot.
His cyberform is
a large scarlet
fire engine.

Firefighter's
helmet

Strong but silent
No Autobird ever hears Heatwave squawk. He just stares and stares and stares – especially when a robot cracks a joke!

Heatwave is always first on the scene if an engine overheats.

His strong fire engine is great for smashing into Deceptihog vehicles head-on.
The pig robots will suffer a major frag and collapse in a nano-klik!

Supreme showdown

Optimus Prime Bird is gearing up for a mighty battle!

It is time to stop the pigs poaching the Egg-bots once and for all.

Megatron tries to shoot Optimus, but he rams into the pig's side.

The naughty porker has a tantrum, and Optimus wins the battle!

The Autobirds have saved the Egg-bots from the pigs – for now! But can they catch the Egg-bots before they all wreck Piggy Island?

Quiz

1. What do the Egg-bots turn the plants and rocks into?

2. What colour does the EggSpark glow?

3. Which member of the Deceptihogs is this?

4. What does Dark Megatron Pig want to do with the Egg-bots?

5. Who is the leader of the Autobirds?

6. What colour is
Bumblebee Bird?

7. Which Autobird
has a light but very
strong chassis?

8. Which Autobird
is very clumsy?

9. What vehicle does Grey Slam
Grimlock Bird turn into?

10. What colour is Heatwave
the Fire-Bot Bird's fire engine?

1. Robotic objects, 2. Blue, 3. Dark Megatron Pig, 4. Eat them, 5. Optimus Prime Bird,
6. Yellow, 7. Bumblebee Bird, 8. Grey Slam Grimlock Bird, 9. A trike, 10. Red.

Glossary

afterburners fiery boosters that increase a robot's speed

astrosecond a short amount of time

audioreceptors a robot's ears

chassis a robot's body

communicates shares information like thoughts, feelings and ideas with others

cunning tricky or clever

faceplate a covering that protects a robot's face

frag an error in a robot's system

henpecked bossed around or nagged

nano-klik a short amount of time

optics a robot's eyes

poach steal

short-circuit when electricity stops flowing properly

vocal processor a robot's voice

Index

DK

Here are some other DK Readers you might enjoy.

Angry Birds™ *Star Wars*™ II: Path to the Pork Side
Can Redkin Skywalker resist the power of the Pork Side?
Join the young Jedi Bird on his journey!

Angry Birds™ *Star Wars*™: Lard Vader's Villains
Meet Lard Vader and the Empire Pigs
as they try to take control of the galaxy.

The LEGO® Movie: Awesome Adventures
Meet Emmet and join him on his extraordinary
quest to save the universe.

LEGO® Legends of Chima™: Heroes' Quest
Join the heroes of Chima™ as they set out on
a dangerous mission to save their land.

Star Wars™ The Legendary Yoda
Yoda is a famous and wise Jedi. Learn all about
his legendary battles and how he uses the Force.

LEGO® Hero Factory: The Brain Wars
It's heroes vs. evil Brains when mind-controlled
beasts invade Makuhero City.